Read all of
Bella Baxter's Adventures:

Aladdin Paperbacks
Published by Simon & Schuster

Bella Baxter # 2

Bella Baxter
and the
Itchy
Disaster

Jane B. Mason & Sarah Hines Stephens
Illustrated by John Shelley

Aladdin Paperbacks
New York London Toronto Sydney

To Nora, a chicken crazy girl
—J. B. M. and S. H. S.

ALADDIN PAPERBACKS
An imprint of Simon & Schuster Children's Publishing Division
1230 Avenue of the Americas, New York, NY 10020
Text copyright © 2005 by Jane B. Mason and Sarah Hines Stephens
Illustrations copyright © 2005 by John Shelley
All rights reserved, including the right of reproduction in whole or
in part in any form.
Designed by Debra Sfetsios
The text of this book was set in Baskerville Book
Printed in the United States of America
First Aladdin Paperbacks edition December 2005
2 4 6 8 10 9 7 5 3 1
Library of Congress Control Number 2004118396
ISBN-13: 978-0-689-86281-6
ISBN-10: 0-689-86281-4

Bella Baxter # 2

Bella Baxter
and the
Itchy
Disaster

CHAPTER 1

Lonely Pastry

Bella Baxter gazed at the buffet table. She was looking at the chocolate croissant. It was from Bruno's Bakery. It looked sweet and sticky, and lonely. It looked like it *wanted* Bella to eat it. But not all of the guests at Sea Inn had eaten. And Bella knew the rules. Guests ate first.

Sometimes there were leftover pastries. When that happened, Bella could have them. Or at least play Rock, Paper, Scissors with her dad for them. (Luckily Barnaby Baxter always split his winnings with his daughter.) But if the pastries were gone, it was cereal city.

Maybe the last guests would be dieters. Bella moved the fruit salad in front of the pastries. She stacked the dirty dishes. She straightened the newspapers. Then she wiped the tables. Finally she sat down on the stairs to wait.

It felt good to sit. Life had been busy since Sea Inn opened for business. Of course, things were busy before Sea Inn opened too. The old house was in lousy shape when Bella and her family arrived. Turning it into a bed-and-breakfast was no piece of cake—or pastry, for that matter.

Luckily for her parents, Bella was a girl of action. She knew where to get help. The local library was the perfect place to research house repair. And to make a new friend. Because that's where she met Trudy. Trudy was quick with a card catalog and even quicker with her tools. It took a lot of hard work. But working together they'd gotten Sea Inn ready just in time.

Bella bit her thumbnail. She wished she were with Trudy right now. Bella needed help again.

She'd gotten a new idea from one of her mom's books. It said that great bed-and-breakfasts made people feel right at home.

That got Bella thinking. And now she knew what she had to do. She had to make Sea Inn feel like each guest's home! And to do that she'd need to know all about where each guest lived. She'd need to know their hobbies and interests. And she'd need to know it *before* they arrived.

And that meant she needed to do research—library research.

Bella slipped into the front hall. She opened the guest registry. In just three days Sea Inn's most important guest, Dr. Frederick Fauna, would arrive. The doctor was a famous botanist from England—definitely a subject worthy of research. And the perfect guest to receive Bella's special welcome.

Bella picked up a pen and made a quick list of things to do. She didn't have any paper, so she wrote on the palm of her hand:

Clear dishes.
Strip beds.
Sweep stairs.
Begin research.

A rumbling sound interrupted Bella's list making. Was that her stomach? She peeked through the door into the dining room.

Mr. and Mrs. Nelson had finally come to breakfast. Their backs were to Bella. They completely blocked the buffet table. Bella couldn't see a single buttery flake of croissant. But she could hear what they were saying.

"Isn't this lovely?" Mrs. Nelson crooned.

"Mmmph," Mr. Nelson agreed. Bella saw his head bob up and down.

"I don't know what to try first!" Mrs. Nelson bubbled. "It all looks so good."

Mrs. Nelson's mouth sounded full. Bella crossed her fingers.

"This croissant is so buttery it melts in your mouth!" she exclaimed.

Bella let out the breath she'd been holding. She uncrossed her fingers. With a sigh she picked up her stack of dishes.

Au revoir, croissant! Bella bid her French pastry good-bye. She pushed open the kitchen door. In her head she added one more thing to her to-do list:

Stop by Bruno's Bakery.

CHAPTER 2

Plant Plan

Shredded Nuggets plunked into Bella's cereal bowl. They sounded dusty. Bella added milk. They still tasted dry.

Oh well, Bella thought. *At least it will keep me going until I get to Bruno's.*

Nellie Baxter was at the sink. She was splashing and clinking her way through the morning dishes. And she was humming!

Bella's ears perked up. It had been ages since she'd heard her mom hum. Moving to Sea Inn had stressed Nellie out. Way out. Even her fantastic cooking had taken a nosedive. Bella crunched on a Shredded Nugget. Compared to some of her mom's recent food disasters, they tasted great.

Bella hummed along between bites. It was good to have her regular mom back. Regular mom hummed. She smiled. She laughed. And most important, she cooked like she used to.

"Can you take the compost out when you're done?" Nellie asked.

Bella's grin faded. Her back-to-normal mom gave her lots of chores, too. Bella's to-do list was already l-o-n-g. And she *had* to get to the library!

Bella popped the last shred of nugget into her mouth. The name *Frederick Fauna* spun around in her head. How was she going to welcome him? What would make a plant scientist feel at home?

Bella carried her bowl to the sink. She grabbed the compost bucket. It was full of slimy food scraps and coffee grounds. Bella's dad always said all that slimy stuff was priceless. Those food scraps just needed a few months in

a big stinky pile of worms and other creepy crawlies. After that, they made a supervitamin shake for his garden. Barnaby Baxter was passionate about his garden.

Bella picked up the bucket carefully. She walked slowly to the front porch. After rounding the house she scampered down the steps to the backyard.

The front of Sea Inn had flower beds, an herb garden, and two patches of lawn. The back was wild. The woods practically grew up to the porch. There were paths leading all over. The one Bella was on led to an old shed circled in chicken wire. Inside the wire was the compost pile.

"Here you go, worms," Bella said. She tipped the bucket upside down. The slimy gunk plunked onto the pile next to a patch of pretty purple flowers.

"I guess you wildflowers like this compost stuff, too." Bella leaned down to get a closer look. She had never seen the tiny flowers before. They were adorable, so she picked a few.

Suddenly Bella stood up straight. She dropped

her bucket. She looked around at all of the plants growing wild around her. "That's it!" shouted. "I can fill Dr. Fauna's room with plants!"

Bella grabbed the bucket and swung it around. Still swinging, she skipped back up the path. Her plan was perfect! Dr. Fauna would feel right at home surrounded by plants. After all, they were his life's work!

Bella hadn't gotten far when she noticed another pretty plant by some birch trees. It had shiny rosy leaves that grew in groups of three. She picked a branch. She stopped again, for a red-and-yellow flower with long pointy petals. And finally a tiny yellow blossom that was growing nestled between two rocks.

Bella's mind raced. She pictured all kinds of plants in vases on Dr. Fauna's windowsill. She could even label them! ITTY-BITTY PURPLE PRETTIES. SHINY TINY LEAF TRIO. It would be fun to think up her own names. But Dr. Fauna was a botanist. He would definitely be more interested in the plants' real names.

Bella clutched her bouquet and ran the rest of the way to the house. She didn't know the real names of any of the plants she was holding. Luckily for Dr. Fauna, research was her specialty!

CHAPTER 3

Too Much to Do

Bella gave a last tug and the fitted sheet slipped off the corner of the mattress. *Thud!* Both she and the sheet landed in a pile on the floor. Bella brushed herself off. Her mind was not exactly on her chores. In fact, she was trying to think of a way to get out of them.

She staggered out of the room carrying a huge pile of sheets. Step by step she made her way down three flights of stairs. The washing machine lived in the basement. Getting there without tripping wasn't easy, but she did it. Bella dropped her pile on the floor as the washer whirred to a stop.

"Perfect timing." Bella's dad dumped a heap of

towels next to her sheets. "This poor machine never gets a break." Bella's dad smiled and shook his head. This was Bella's chance.

"I know how it feels," she said. Bella slumped against the washer and gazed up at her dad through her eyelashes.

Barnaby bit his lip. Bella stifled a grin. Her dad was softening!

"Well, Bell, you have been helping us an awful lot lately," he said slowly.

"And it *is* summer vacation," Bella reminded him.

"Why don't you take the rest of the day off, pumpkin? I think your mom and I can keep things running without you for a day."

"Great!" Bella said. She gave her dad a quick peck on the

cheek. Then she zoomed up the stairs.

Five minutes later Bella was galloping toward Sandyport Public Library. Her only stop was Bruno's for a chocolate croissant. But by the time it was only a buttery memory, she hit the library steps. She was already wondering what to look up first.

"This is an unusual specimen," she imagined herself saying to Dr. Fauna. *"It only grows in the shade of Sea Inn."*

Bella pushed open the heavy double doors.

"Bella!" Trudy practically shouted. A man reading nearby looked up sternly. Trudy scowled at him but lowered her voice.

"How have you been? How's the Inn? Need more books on roofing?" she whispered.

"Great. Great. And not today," Bella replied. She wanted to get down to business. "Today I need to learn about local plants."

"Fascinating subject," Trudy said. "One of my favorites." Trudy tucked a pencil behind her ear. She closed the book she was reading: *Positively*

Poultry. Then she headed for the stacks. "The five eighties are what we need. Ah, here."

Trudy pulled books off the shelves as quickly as Bella could read the titles. First came *Every Single Thing That Grows on the Eastern Seaboard. Know Where It Grows* was next. And finally a thick one called *The Succinct Guide to Succulents of the Northeast.*

"There's a start!" Trudy said. She dusted off her hands. Staggering and grateful, Bella took her pile to a table. A minute later she was engrossed in a chapter about wildflowers.

She found the little purple pretties. They were violets. But there were loads of different kinds of violets.

Ugh. Bella rested her forehead on page 451 of *Know Where It Grows*. Maybe her brain would just suck the information in through her forehead. There was no way she could remember all of the plants well enough to find them herself. She needed to be out in the woods, not sitting in the library.

Dr. Fauna has probably been studying plants his whole life, Bella thought. What could she learn in three days that would impress him? Bella closed the book with a loud *thump*.

The grumpy man frowned. Bella felt her eyes well up with tears. She turned away from the grouch and saw a friendly face. Trudy's.

The librarian's red lips were pursed.

"What you need is some field research," Trudy said. "We need to get to the woods, get back to nature."

Almost immediately Bella's eyes dried up. Trudy read her thoughts as easily as any book. And she'd said *we*.

"You'll help me?" Bella asked.

Trudy nodded. "I'll be at your place at five o'clock sharp."

CHAPTER 4

Not a Peep

Bella sat on the Sea Inn porch all afternoon. Her nose was buried in the books she'd checked out. She learned that foxgloves only bloomed every other year. And that their seeds were used in heart medicine. Who knew?

"What're you reading, gumdrop?" her dad asked. He was carrying a basket of line-dried sheets.

"I'm learning about local plants," Bella answered. She didn't look up. The chapter on vines and climbers was fascinating!

"An excellent subject!" Barnaby replied. "Can I help?"

Bella let the book fall to her lap. "No, thanks," she said slowly. She was proud of her plan. But she wanted to keep it a secret. If she told her parents she was planning a surprise, they might worry. Parents were like that.

Barnaby tousled his daughter's hair and headed into the house. Bella turned back to her book. Up next was a section on unusual edible plants. Bella felt a tingle run up her spine. Dr. Fauna would love these!

The edibles caused more than a spine tingle. They caused a tummy rumble. It was four thirty— time for a snack.

"Hi Mom." Bella opened the fridge and waved. She was craving something . . . leafy. "Do we have any purslane?"

"Purslane?" Nellie repeated. She wrinkled her forehead. "What's that?"

"It's an edible succulent. Grows almost anywhere. Forests, dirt parking lots, flower beds. Many people consider it a weed. But it is actually quite delicious in soups and salads."

"Fascinating," Nellie replied. She shook her head slightly. "But I'm afraid we're fresh out."

Bella reached for a carrot and a bottle of ranch dressing. Maybe she and Trudy could find some purslane in the woods.

"Trudy's coming over. We're going to go for a walk in the woods, okay?"

"Sure, sweetie," Nellie said. "Be back for dinner."

By five o'clock Bella had finished her carrot and the next chapter. Then it was five-oh-five. Then five ten. Then five twenty. Bella was hungry again and Trudy was nowhere to be seen.

Bella went into the kitchen and dialed Trudy's number. It rang three times before Trudy picked up.

"Hi Trudy, it's Bella," Bella said.

"Bella!" Trudy said. She sounded a little frantic. "I'm so glad you called. I need you over here right away."

Bella was stunned. That was what *she* was going to say. It sounded like Trudy had forgotten all about their date! But it also sounded like Trudy needed her.

"Can I go to Trudy's?" Bella asked her mom.

Nellie nodded. "Dinner's at seven," she reminded her.

"I'll be right over," Bella said. She'd never been to Trudy's, but it was only a couple of blocks away. She wrote down the address. Then she hung up the phone and headed out the door.

As it turned out, Bella did not need the address. She would have known Trudy's house anywhere! It had wide blue and yellow stripes on one side. The garage was covered in pink polka dots. And the door was bright green! Six rocking chairs with comfy-looking pillows stood on the porch. And the garden overflowed with wild-looking flowers and plants. Bella recognized cosmos and petunias from her reading.

Before Bella could knock on the door Trudy opened it. A hat covered her spiky hair. She wore a beige trench coat with the collar up.

"Good, you're here," she said. "We've got to get to the post office. It's already closed, but Sam usually works late on Thursdays. Come on!"

Trudy sprinted down the walk. Bella hurried after her.

"My cousin Earl just called," Trudy explained. "He sent me a package and called to see how I liked it. Said it was due to arrive yesterday. Only I didn't get it! Those poor babies!" Trudy cried. "I hope they're okay!"

Trudy was talking fast and walking faster. Bella had a hard time keeping up. What babies?

"Ah! Here we are!" Trudy exclaimed. "Thank goodness the lights are still on." Trudy pounded on the post office door.

A man in a postal uniform came to answer it. He smiled when he saw Trudy.

"Well if it isn't my favorite librarian," the man said.

"Hi Sam," Trudy replied. "Do you have a package for me?" Her eyes were wide.

"I'm not sure," Sam replied. "I was out for most of the afternoon. I had a dentist's appointment. I was just sorting through the parcels. Why don't we just have a look?" He smiled at Bella.

The threesome made their way to a giant room at the back of the post office. A big mail cart full of letters stood right in the middle. Packages of all shapes and sizes lined the far shelves.

Trudy scanned the shelves. She seemed to know just what she was looking for.

"There!" she cried. She pointed to a shoebox-size package on a high shelf. It had several holes in it and was labeled LIVE ANIMALS. HANDLE WITH CARE.

Bella's eyes widened. Live animals!

Sam climbed onto a stepladder. Very carefully, he lifted the box down.

"It has your name on it, all right," Sam said. "Here you go." He handed the box to Trudy.

Trudy hugged the box like it was a long-lost friend. She put her ear up to one of the

holes and listened. Then she grinned.

"Listen," she held the box up to Bella. Bella leaned in close.

"Peep!" went the box. "Peep! Peep!"

CHAPTER 5

Peep, Peep, Peep!

"Thanks so much, Sam," Trudy said. She leaned forward and gave him a peck on the cheek. Sam blushed.

"Anytime, Trudy," Sam mumbled.

Trudy turned to Bella. "Let's get these babies home. They need food and water, pronto!" Trudy walked home just as fast as she had walked to the post office. Bella didn't have a chance to catch her breath. Or to ask what was peeping. It was all she could do to keep up. She was *very* relieved when they got back to Trudy's.

When Bella stepped inside the living room, her jaw dropped. The outside of Trudy's house was interesting. The inside was even better! Wacky statues sat on bookshelves and side tables. Colorful masks and paintings hung on the walls. There wasn't a lot of furniture. Giant pillows covered the floor.

"I like your house!" Bella said. She'd never seen so many different kinds of things in one place. It was like a museum!

"Thanks." Trudy set her package on a table. Then she gently opened it.

Bella almost fell over when she saw what was inside. Baby chicks! A *lot* of baby chicks! She tried counting, but the box was really full. Plus, the chicks started flopping around like crazy when they saw the light.

Trudy slumped down into a chair.

"Thank goodness they're all alive," she said. "Twenty-five healthy babies."

"Twenty-five!" Bella echoed. "Wow!"

"They have to send that many in the mail," Trudy explained. "They're so small they need each other to stay warm."

Trudy gazed at the tiny, fluffy chicks. Then she

sat up with a start. "We have to make them a home, of course. And they need to eat and drink!"

Trudy hurried away. A few minutes later she came back with a large wooden crate. Inside was a desk lamp with a red bulb. There was also a bag of wood shavings. And a water jug with a little tube sticking out of the bottom.

"I guess you've done this before," Bella said.

Trudy nodded. "But not in a long time," she

confessed. "Chickens take a lot of work. But just look at them!" She reached down and touched a tiny, peeping fluff ball.

"Can I hold one?" Bella asked.

"Of course," Trudy replied.

Holding her breath, Bella lifted a tiny chick into her palm. It weighed almost nothing! And its fuzzy body was softer than rabbit fur. Bella petted the chick gently with one finger. She could feel its fast-beating heart.

Trudy spread wood shavings on the bottom of the crate. Then she laid newspaper on top. Finally she plugged in the lamp and clipped it to the side of the crate.

"This will give them light and heat," she explained. She peered into the box full of chicks. "Aha!" she said. In the corner was a small container. "They sent some starter food along."

Trudy sprinkled some feed on top of the newspaper. "This will make it easier for the little peepers to find their food," she said. "Later we can use a regular chicken feeder."

Bella was impressed. Trudy obviously knew a lot about raising chickens.

The chicks were perking up more and more. They were peeping like crazy. Some of them were even trying to climb out of the box!

"Peep! Peep!" the tiny chick in Bella's hand squeaked faintly. Gently she set the chick down in its new home.

"And now for water," Trudy said. She looked up at Bella. "That's the tricky part."

Trudy went into the kitchen. A minute later she came back. She was carrying a small bowl of clean water, a spoon, and a sugar bowl.

"We put a little sugar in their water to give them extra energy. They need it after their long trip," Trudy explained. She picked up a peeping chick and dipped its beak into the water. Then she set it in the crate.

"You try it," Trudy encouraged.

Bella reached for another chick. This one seemed even tinier and softer than the first. Very gently she dipped its beak in the water.

Then she set it down in the crate, too.

One by one Trudy and Bella gave each chick a drink. They were so small and fuzzy. Bella was in love with them all.

When they were done Trudy stood up. She jingled her library keys. "I think we need to do a little chicken research," she said.

"Right now?" Bella asked. She was surprised. It was getting dark. She had to be home for dinner. And what about their plant plans? "I was really hoping to—"

Trudy's hand flew to her mouth. "The plants!" she said. "Oh, Bella. I forgot all about the plants! I'm so sorry!"

Trudy straightened up. "Come with me," she said.

Bella followed Trudy down a flight of stairs. The basement was packed! Bella spotted all kinds of interesting stuff. There was a big pile of small canning jars. A pinball machine stood in one corner. A puppet theater looked ready for a show. And of course there were boxes and boxes of books. Trudy rummaged through the mess.

"Here!" she finally exclaimed. She opened a dusty trunk. Out came a pair of mining helmets with headlamps. Then a butterfly net and some old tin buckets.

Bella giggled. Trudy always made her feel better.

"You don't like my helmets?" Trudy asked. She pretended to be hurt.

"They're terrific!" Bella replied. "But it's kind of late. I told my parents I'd be home for dinner."

Trudy checked her watch. "Right you are, *ma chérie*," she said. She took the helmet off. "Let's go tomorrow instead." She led Bella back upstairs. "I'll come as soon as I'm off work. Okay?"

"Deal." Bella leaned over the crate-house and blew the little chicks a kiss. Then she gave Trudy a hug.

"See you tomorrow!" Bella bounded out the door. She skipped all the way home.

CHAPTER 6

Baby Care

"They are soooo cute!" Bella said. She forked up some scrambled eggs. "And so fluffy!" She was having breakfast with her parents in the kitchen. Since there were only two guests at Sea Inn, they had time to have a quick bite together. Bella had told her parents about the chicks the night before. But she couldn't stop talking about them. "And they have these tiny black eyes. There are twenty-five of them. Did I tell you that?"

"Twice." Barnaby Baxter chewed his toast. "Did they really come in the mail?"

Bella nodded. "In a regular box. Only it had holes, and the outside said 'Live Animals. Handle With Care.' So I guess it wasn't really that regular." Bella scratched her wrist. It had been a little itchy since she woke up.

"That Trudy is full of surprises," Nellie said.

"Kind of like someone else we know," Bella's dad said. He raised his eyebrows at Bella.

Bella grinned. Her dad always said it was better to be full of surprises than full of beans.

The phone rang. Giving her wrist another scratch, Bella picked it up. It was Trudy. "Bella!" she said. "We have an urgent chick situation. Can you come to my house at lunch?"

"Sure." Bella scratched her elbow. It was a little itchy, too.

"You're a lifesaver, toots," Trudy said. "I'll meet you there at twelve sharp."

"Okay," Bella said. "And we're still picking plants tonight, right?"

"Absolutely," Trudy agreed.

Bella made the guest beds in record time. She

hung out the clean towels. And she put the little bars of fancy soap in the bathrooms. Then she put fresh flowers in the rooms—except for Dr. Fauna's, of course. He would be getting some very special bouquets!

At exactly twelve o'clock Bella pushed open Trudy's bright green door. Trudy was sitting at the table holding a chick.

"They're just like babies!" she exclaimed. "They don't wear diapers. But we have to wipe their tiny bottoms!"

Bella laughed out loud. She wasn't sure Trudy was serious. "We do?" she asked.

Trudy nodded. She pointed to the supplies on the table. There was a bowl of warm water and a pile of cotton balls. Next to them was a book on chick care. A freshly lined crate sat on the floor.

"They're pasting up," Trudy said. She looked straight at Bella over the tops of her glasses. "When they poop it dries and sticks to their rumps like paste. It's messy. And worse, it traps their next poop inside!"

Bella scratched her arm. It was itching now, too. "That sounds terrible!" she said. But she wasn't sure about wiping chick bums.

"Gross, huh?" Trudy grinned. She looked seriously at Bella. "Are you ready for a little poop patrol?"

Bella pulled out a chair and sat down. She had watched her aunt change her cousin's dirty diaper plenty of times. Yuck-ola. But the chicks—and Trudy—needed her.

Bella exhaled slowly. "Count me in," she said.

Trudy smiled. She dipped a cotton ball in water. She held one of the chicks around the middle. Quickly she wiped its bottom. A tiny brown glob came off. But that was all. Nothing too nasty.

Trudy set the freshly wiped chick in the clean crate.

"Peep! Peep!" it said.

"You're welcome." Bella giggled.

Trudy picked up another chick and wiped its bottom. Bella watched closely. She didn't want to hurt the chicks.

"Okay, I'm ready," she announced. She held a
chick as gently as she could without dropping it.
She held her breath. And she wiped its downy
behind. It wiggled a little, but didn't complain.

"There you go, little fella," Bella said. She put

the baby chicken next to the other two.

"Three down, twenty-two to go," Trudy announced.

Trudy and Bella wiped bottom after bottom. When they were done they gave the babies fresh food and water. Then Bella clipped the heat lamp to the side of the crate.

"Peep, peep, peep!"

Bella looked closely at the chicks. Some of them had already pooped!

"Mission accomplished," Trudy said. "Now, how about some lunch? I've got cold noodle salad, strawberries, and lemonade."

Bella's stomach growled. Wiping chick bottoms was gross. But it had not ruined her appetite!

CHAPTER 7

Into the Woods!

The grandfather clock in the front hall bonged six times. Six o'clock—time for Trudy. Bella sat on the stairs. A pair of clippers and a bucket rested at her feet. She scraped her arm up and down the ridge of the bucket. It felt good. She scraped it again and wondered if she should worry about Trudy. She knew it wasn't easy to take care of twenty-five new babies.

Bella didn't have to wonder long. At six thirty-two there was a knock on the front door.

"Mom, I'm leaving!" Bella called. She pulled the heavy door open and grinned. As usual,

Trudy was totally prepared. Her tool belt held three pairs of clippers and a butterfly net. She wore a crazy hat with netting that covered her face. And she carried a bucket of water.

Trudy noticed Bella eyeing her hood. "It's for Bee Charming," she explained. "But I think it will work on plants. Don't you?"

Bella wasn't sure if plants needed charming. But the hood looked good, so she just nodded. "How are the chicks?" she asked.

"My little puff balls!" Trudy said with a smile. "They're busy pecking and pooping away. They're doing just dandy thanks to you."

"Hi Trudy." Nellie stepped into the hall. "Bella told me you got chickens in the mail."

"They arrived in the nick of time." Trudy nodded solemnly. "Ah, there's nothing like getting a box of peeping fluff in the mail."

Bella scratched a figure eight around her freckles. *What would it be like to be mailed somewhere?*

"Except maybe getting a snake," Trudy added thoughtfully.

"You get snakes in the mail, too?" Nellie asked. Bella stopped scratching.

"Just once. From my friend Delaney. She sent a constrictor from Brazil. During its hibernation period, thank goodness." Trudy grinned. "I'd love to tell you more, but we have work to do." Trudy pulled a book out of her hip pocket: *The Budding Botanist's Guide to All Things Green and Leafy*.

"What are you two up to?" Bella's mom asked.

"Nothing!" Bella said quickly. A little too quickly. Her mom looked suspicious.

Bella grabbed Trudy's hand and pulled her out the door. Fast.

"Bye," she yelled over her shoulder.

"I can't believe you used to have a snake!" Bella led Trudy down the path behind Sea Inn. "How long did you keep it?"

"About two years," Trudy said. "But New York was too cold for Lady Diamond. So I took her back to the rain forest." Trudy bent low just beyond the compost pile. She clipped a green-and-white leafed plant. "You know, I collected plants on that trip, too."

"You did?" Bella asked. It seemed like Trudy had done everything. Bella squatted down by a tiny red flower. She picked it and put it in the bucket. Then she thumbed through the guide to find its name.

"We collected plant samples for scientists back home. They experimented with them to make new medicines. I always got the best ones because my friend Sal told me where to look. He's a witch doctor."

Bella stopped looking for the red flower in the guidebook. It was taking too long. She needed to do more collecting. She could tag the samples later.

"What's over there by that tree?" Trudy pointed. "That blue flower. Oh, we have to get that!"

"And that!" Bella pointed to a tall yellow blossom. "I want one of *everything*."

Trudy and Bella darted from flower to flower like busy bees. Soon their buckets and arms were full. *Really* full. And it was getting dark.

"I should have brought those mining helmets after all!" Trudy said through her huge bouquet.

"I think we have enough," Bella panted. She was wondering how she was going to identify everything in time. Dr. Fauna was arriving tomorrow! She wondered something else, too. How was she going to scratch her itchy arm with her hands full of plants?

CHAPTER 8

That Little Itch

"Ptooey." Trudy spat the hat netting out of her mouth. She set her heavy bucket on the porch with a slosh. It was filled with branches and leaves and stems and blossoms.

"I think we really did get one of everything!" Bella said. She slumped down on the stairs and gave her arm a good scratch.

"I wish I could stay and help you look them all up," Trudy said. "But I have to get back and feed my chicks."

Trudy was just like a mother hen. But Bella didn't mind. She had already helped a lot.

"*Au revoir, ma petite!*" Trudy called over her shoulder.

Bella hauled the buckets upstairs as quietly as she could. Then she snuck back down. She needed lots of small bottles. Luckily her dad was always buying little vases at garage sales.

Bella lined the vases up on Dr. Fauna's windowsill. She filled them with water. Then she found each plant in her book and wrote its name on a piece of masking tape.

GIANT HYSSOP, she printed carefully. She wrapped the tape around a droopy purple blossom. GOLDEN ZIZIA she wrote on the next piece of tape.

The grandfather clock in the hall bonged eight times. Bella turned on the light by Dr. Fauna's bed and looked for a picture of a yellow cone-shaped flower. She scratched her arm as she looked. There it was. Butterflybush.

Bella yawned and stretched. She surveyed the bottles and vases. They were all full, but there were still a few things in the buckets. Bella didn't want to throw them out. But she was too tired to look them up. Then she remembered a picture her mom had shown her of a bed strewn with flower petals. Perfect! She could put the rest on the bed.

Carefully Bella plucked shiny green leaves from a woody stem—the pretty ones that grew in threes. She tossed them in the air so they fell onto the clean white sheets. She stood back to admire her work. The room was perfect!

Both windowsills were lined with plant-filled bottles. The dresser held half a dozen vases. And the bed was covered in beautiful leaves. Bella crossed her arms and gave her elbow a satisfied scratch. Mission accomplished!

All night Bella tossed and turned. She was too excited about her plan to sleep. And too itchy. Bella's hand itched. Her arm itched. Her elbow itched. And now her neck itched too.

While Bella scratched she thought about Dr. Fauna. Would he like his room? Would he feel like he was sleeping in the woods? Maybe she

and Trudy had found some rare plant species. Maybe Dr. Fauna would write about her in an important paper. Bella pictured herself on stage in an auditorium of famous scientists.

"I owe it all to a little B & B called Sea Inn—and the brilliant Bella Baxter!" Dr. Fauna would say.

Bella fell asleep to the sound of imaginary

applause. She woke up to the sound of real rattling juice glasses.

Bella jumped out of bed. She gave her neck a good scratch. She pulled on her green shorts and the shirt with the leaf prints she made at camp.

Dressed and ready to go, Bella hurried downstairs. Nobody was in the dining room. Bella was too excited to even count the croissants.

"Good morning!" Bella chirped. She pushed open the swinging kitchen door.

"Good morning," Barnaby said. He lifted a tray of coffee cups over her head.

"Oh, Bella," Nellie Baxter said. She was whisking a bowl of eggs. "The plants and flowers you put in Dr. Fauna's room are lovely. But I took the leaves off the sheets. They looked too . . . messy," Bella's mom smiled. "Hope you don't mind."

Bella grinned. Her mom liked her surprise! "That's okay, Mom," she said.

Just then Bella heard a car in the driveway. Dr. Fauna was already here!

Bella peeked through the curtain. A tall man stepped out of a bright yellow rental car. He had gray hair. But Dr. Fauna did not move like an old man. He practically bounced out of the small car. And when he looked at Sea Inn he smiled broadly.

"Excuse me." Mr. and Mrs. Nelson had just come down to breakfast. "Do you have any more of those delicious pastries?" Mrs. Nelson asked.

"Here you go." Bella held out a plate of Bruno's best. She didn't even cringe when the Nelsons took the good ones. She was too busy listening to Dr. Fauna check in.

"Your room is upstairs. First door on the right," Nellie directed.

Bella put down the pastries. Very quietly, she slipped out of the dining room and followed Dr. Fauna upstairs. She felt like a spy. The tall man opened the door to his room and set his bag on the bed. Bella thought she heard him gasp. Did he like the plants?

She walked past his door as slowly as she could. She had to see what he was doing! Dr. Fauna dug around in his bag. He pulled out a small glasses case. With his glasses perched on

his nose he began to read the masking-tape tags.

Bella's steps got smaller and smaller. Soon she was barely moving at all.

The doctor spun around and saw her. "What lovely foliage!" he exclaimed. "Did you do this?"

Bella beamed.

"It is a veritable feast of local botany! I shall feel as though I am sleeping in my own private greenhouse!"

It was exactly the reaction Bella had hoped for. But she suddenly felt a little shy. "I got them in the woods. Behind the inn," she said softly.

"A place I must certainly explore," Dr. Fauna nodded. "And I can begin right here in my own room!" He pushed his half-glasses up his nose. He studied another specimen. "This beeblossom is an unusual shade," he noted. "I've never seen anything quite like it."

Things were going better than Bella hoped! She nodded and tried to listen to Dr. Fauna. Unfortunately, her elbow was really, *really* itching.

She scratched it behind her back. But the itch was working its way up her arm. And it was starting to feel bumpy.

"I can take you out back when I finish my chores," Bella volunteered. She stepped out of the room and raced toward hers. She needed a good scratch!

Bella tried to ignore the itching while she gathered the laundry. It wasn't easy. As she was passing through the kitchen the phone rang. Bella shifted the pile of towels and picked it up.

"Sea Inn. This is Bella. How can I help you?" Bella answered just the way her mom had told her to.

"Bella! It's Trudy. How'd the foliage sampler go over with the plant doctor?"

"Great!" Bella replied. She tucked the phone under her chin. She scratched the arm holding the towels. She was starting to really worry about the itching. "But I think we might have a problem. I have to look something up in the plant books. Can I call you back?"

"Sure, but make it quick if you can. I'll be holding my breath!"

"I will," Bella promised. She said good-bye and hung up.

Bella clumped down to the basement and dumped the towels by the washer. Then she raced back to her room, scratching all the way. She grabbed *The Budding Botanist's Guide*. She had identified all the plants in Dr. Fauna's room except one: the one with the shiny green leaves. Bella searched through the section on non-flowering plants. She found what she was looking for.

With a groan, Bella threw herself backward onto her bed.

CHAPTER 9

Remedy to the Rescue

Poison ivy! She had covered Dr. Fauna's bed with poison ivy! Bella felt sick to her stomach. Her arm and neck itched like mad. And soon Sea Inn's best guest would be itching to leave!

There was only one thing to do. She had to change Dr. Fauna's sheets. Pronto. She skidded to a stop in front of his door. She put her ear next to it and listened. All was quiet inside. She was in luck! Dr. Fauna had gone out.

Carefully Bella opened the door to Dr. Fauna's room. But before she could look inside she heard a noise. It sounded like a . . . snore.

She peeked in and gasped. Dr. Fauna was taking a nap. And worse, he was lying on the bed. Right where the poison ivy leaves had been!

Bella closed the door and sank to the floor. This was not good. In fact, this was terrible.

Bella was trying to come up with a plan when the phone rang. Trudy! She'd forgotten to call her back. And now she *really* needed to talk to her.

"We have an emergency," Bella said. "I'm coming to the library right now."

"I'll be here, ready and waiting," Trudy said.

Bella grabbed *The Budding Botanist's Guide*. She

hollered to her parents. Itching like mad, she raced out the door.

Trudy was waiting at the information desk. Bella had planned to explain everything carefully. But by the time she got to the library, she was panicked.

"I gave Dr. Fauna poison ivy!" she blurted. She scratched her neck.

One of Trudy's eyebrows shot up over her cat-eye glasses. "Really," she said. She tapped a number-two pencil on her desk.

"Really." Tears welled up in Bella's eyes. "My mom is going to kill me!"

"No, she isn't," Trudy said in her librarian voice. "But that poison ivy might if you keep scratching it like that." Trudy pointed her pencil at the growing red patches on Bella's arm and neck. Bella stuffed her fists in her pockets.

"Don't worry," Trudy said. "My friend Sal taught me something important. There's a remedy for every malady. And most of the time the remedy is growing right nearby."

Trudy flipped through her card catalog. "Mr. Dewey says that six fifteen point five will have our answer." She smiled reassuringly at Bella.

Bella followed Trudy to the 615.5s. They found a remedy book right away. It was called *Heloise Reason's Herbal Remedies for All Seasons*.

Bella looked up poison ivy. Sure enough, the book had a recipe for an herbal salve. "To calm the itch and prevent the rash from spreading," it said. Bella read the recipe aloud.

Trudy recognized most of the ingredients in the recipe. But they still had to collect all the plants and mix them into a salve.

"A salve is like an ointment with healing properties," Trudy explained.

Bella nodded. Her collar rubbed against her poison ivy, scratching it a little. She nodded again. The recipe looked kind of complicated. But she would do anything if it could stop her itching!

Trudy looked around. "It's awfully quiet around here today," she said. "I'll bet Hector could manage the information desk by himself.

Then we can head out to the woods right now!"

Bella watched Trudy disappear behind the stacks. She hoped Hector was in a good mood.

Trudy was back in seconds. And she was smiling. "Let's go," she said.

Ten minutes later Bella and Trudy were collecting plants behind Sea Inn again. They found almost everything the recipe called for: jewelweed, sweet fern, comfrey, and chickweed. From Barnaby's garden they plucked the last ingredient, marigold.

"We need to let them dry a little, just until they're wilted," Trudy said. "Let's take them to my house and lay them in the sun. We can make the salve there."

Bella grimaced. She hadn't realized making salve would take so long. She was wearing her father's gardening gloves to remind her not to scratch. The itching was *bad.* And the thought of Dr. Fauna finding out she poisoned his bed was even worse!

"Don't worry, Bella," Trudy said. She slung an

arm around Bella's shoulder. "Dr. Fauna won't start itching until tomorrow."

Back at Trudy's house, they said a quick hello to the chicks. Then they laid the plants out to dry on Trudy's porch.

"Into the lab!" Trudy said. She led Bella into the kitchen. Trudy loved experimenting with her own lotions and stuff. She had all they needed. And more important, she knew what to do!

"First things first," Trudy said. She pulled a pink bottle from a cupboard. "Calamine. It'll help." Bella spread the pink chalky goop on her arm and neck. It did help. A little.

Then Trudy pulled a Crock-Pot from a high cupboard. She poured some olive oil into it. When the herbs were wilted, Bella put them in the Crock-Pot and turned it on.

"Give it a stir," Trudy said. Bella used a wooden spoon to stir the herbs and oil. She felt a little bit like a scientist.

"It has to cook for a while," Trudy explained. She added some pieces of beeswax. Bella stirred some more while it melted. Then she went to check on the chicks.

They were bigger. Their peeping was getting louder, too. "They're going to outgrow their box," Bella said. Already it looked crowded.

"They grow up so fast." Trudy sighed. They played with the balls of fluff for a while. Then Trudy announced that it was blender time.

In the kitchen Trudy poured the warm herbal oil into a blender. She added some herbs and turned it on. Soon the mixture turned a lovely yellowy green color.

"It won't keep as long with the fresh herbs mixed in," Trudy said. "But it makes the salve a little stronger. Plus, it's prettier."

Bella had to agree.

Trudy drummed her fingers on the counter. "We just need some jars," she murmured.

Bella leaped off her stool. "I know!" she said. She tromped downstairs to the basement. The pile of small canning jars was just where she'd seen it. She carried several upstairs.

"Excellent detective work!" Trudy crowed. She and Bella filled the jars with the ivy salve.

"When it's cool it will harden," Trudy said.

"Do you have any paper? I can make labels," Bella said excitedly. She was feeling a lot better. Their plan to keep Dr. Fauna from an itchy disaster was going to work! And staying busy was keeping her mind off the itching. She sat down at Trudy's desk and wrote: TRY ME! SEA INN'S SPECIAL SALVE. MADE FROM LOCAL PLANTS AND HERBS. She taped it neatly onto a jar.

Trudy nodded approvingly. "Dr. Fauna will love it. Of course, we should test it first."

Trudy spread the still-warm green goo on Bella's arm and neck. It smelled a little funny and familiar. Like hay. But it helped.

"I don't itch!" Bella said, amazed. She wrapped her ungooped arm around Trudy. "Thank you!"

Trudy shook her head. "That's what friends are for. But you should skedaddle. The sooner Dr. Fauna uses his salve, the better." She winked at Bella.

"Right!" Bella agreed. She grabbed her guide and two jars of salve. Then she hurried out the door.

Bella spotted Dr. Fauna in the garden with her dad. They were discussing local shrubs.

Bella raced upstairs. She carefully placed a jar of salve on the shelf above the sink. Then she quickly changed Dr. Fauna's sheets.

Satisfied, she went back downstairs. Her dad and Dr. Fauna were on the porch drinking lemonade.

"Phew, it's hot!" Bella said. She plopped herself

down on a chair. "I think a shower before dinner would be just the thing. Don't you, Dr. Fauna?"

Bella's dad gave his daughter his what-are-you-up-to look. But Dr. Fauna was already on his feet. Taking his last sip of lemonade, he nodded.

"A fine idea," he said. "I think I'll head up right now."

Bella grinned. "I'm sure you'll find your bathroom stocked with all the necessary items," she said.

Bella's dad was staring at her. Hard. Bella got to her feet and followed Dr. Fauna inside. Luckily her dad didn't say anything.

The next half an hour seemed like a year. Bella sat in the parlor, reading. But it took her ten minutes to read one paragraph. She kept listening for Dr. Fauna. Finally he appeared. "I found a most interesting salve in my room," he said slowly. "Did you concoct it yourself, Ms. Baxter?"

"I, uh, had some help," Bella stammered. Did Dr. Fauna know? Was he angry?

"Well, I quite enjoyed it. Especially the strong essence of, was that jewelweed? Rather bitter, but pleasant. And I'm sure I detected marigold."

He looked down at Bella. His eyes were twinkling. Then he reached into his pocket and pulled out a small plastic bag. Inside was a single poison ivy leaf.

"I found this on my bed," he explained. "So I asked your mother to kindly change the sheets before I napped. If I had known you were a botanist *and* a chemist, I would not have bothered. Your salve would have taken care of it, I'm sure."

Dr. Fauna chuckled heartily. Bella giggled. He wasn't mad. He was impressed!

"I think next year I shall come stay for a whole week," Dr. Fauna said. "I would love to explore the area with a local expert like yourself!"

"That would be great," Bella agreed. "There are some really neat plants around here. There's just one thing I should warn you about." She grinned. "You have to watch out for poison ivy!"